Bixby
AND THE VERY BAD IDEA

Published by Redemption Press, PO Box 427, Enumclaw, WA 98022.

Toll-Free (844) 2REDEEM (273-3336)

Redemption Press is honored to present this title in partnership with the author. The views expressed or implied in this work are those of the author. Redemption Press provides our imprint seal representing design excellence, creative content, and high-quality production.

ISBN 13: 978-1-64645-794-6 (paperback)
ISBN: 978-1-951350-62-8 (epub)
Library of Congress Catalog Card Number : 2023914405

Bixby

AND THE VERY BAD IDEA

Written by **Jerri Lien**

Illustrations by **Art Innovations**

In memory of Karen McVay

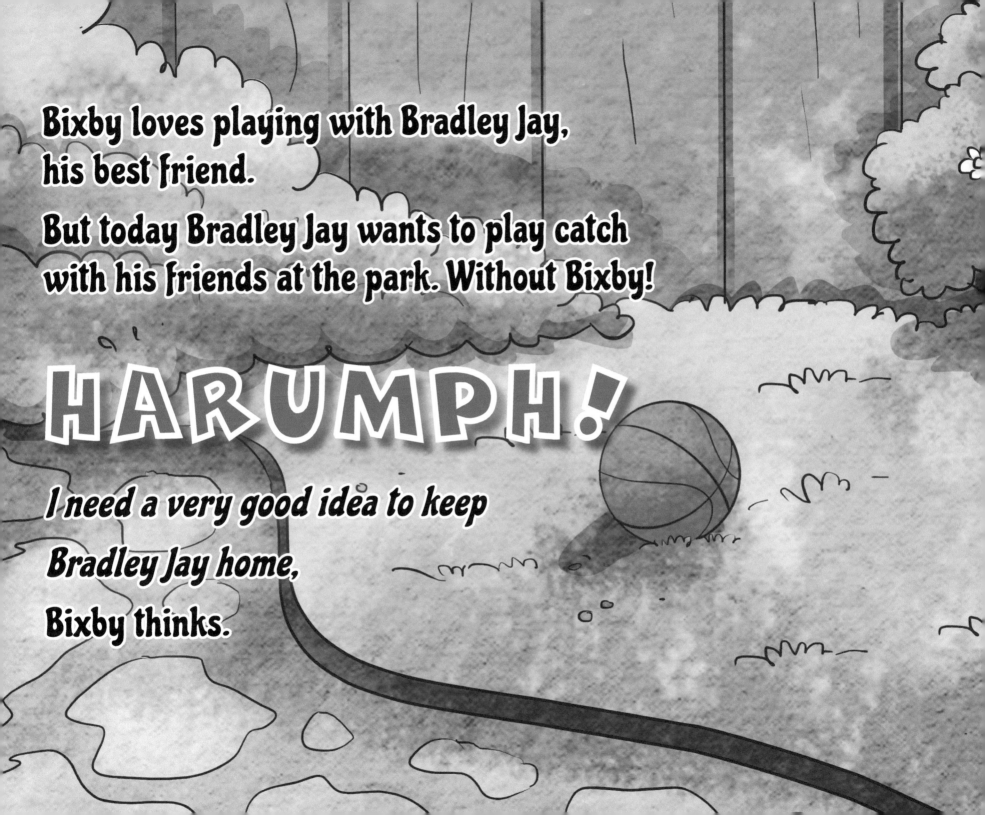

Bixby loves playing with Bradley Jay,
his best friend.

But today Bradley Jay wants to play catch
with his friends at the park. Without Bixby!

HARUMPH!

I need a very good idea to keep

Bradley Jay home,

Bixby thinks.

When Bradley Jay isn't looking, Bixby makes off with his baseball mitt.

"This is a very bad idea!" says Lil Ladybug.

"I just want Bradley Jay to play with me," Bixby says.

"He will be upset that his baseball mitt is missing!" says Lil Ladybug.

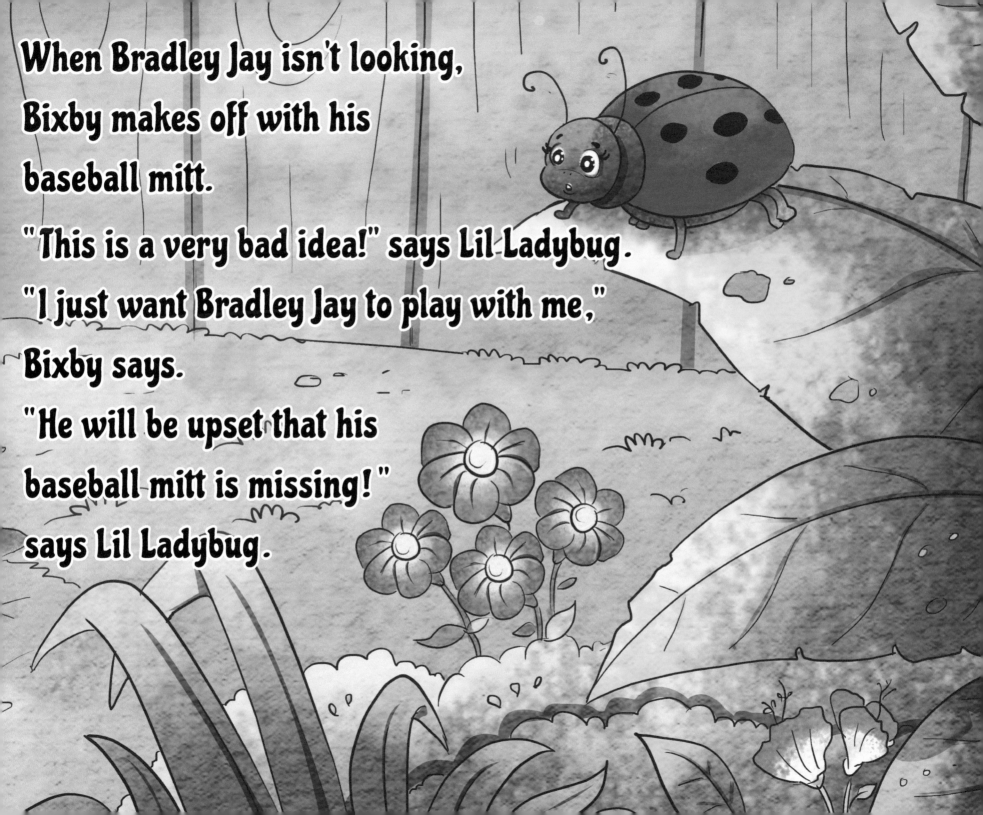

But Bradley Jay does not play with Bixby.

Bixby's tummy gives a twinge.

HARUMPH!

Bixby thinks.

I'll find someone else to play with.

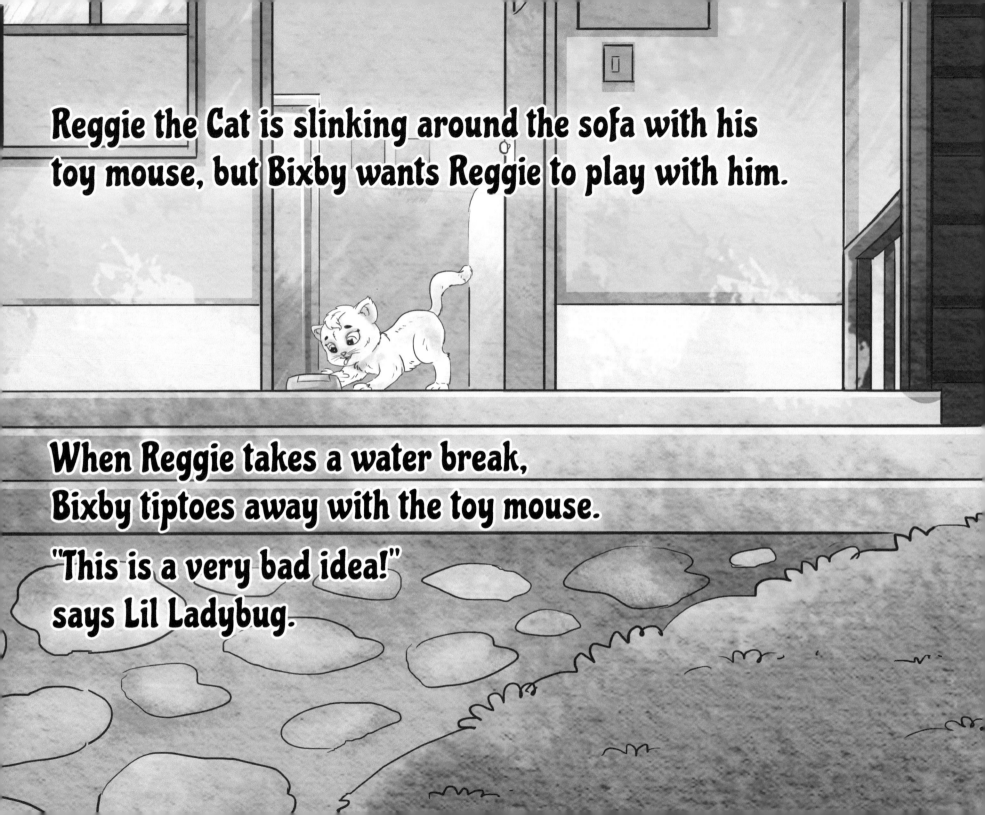

Reggie the Cat is slinking around the sofa with his toy mouse, but Bixby wants Reggie to play with him.

When Reggie takes a water break, Bixby tiptoes away with the toy mouse.

"This is a very bad idea!" says Lil Ladybug.

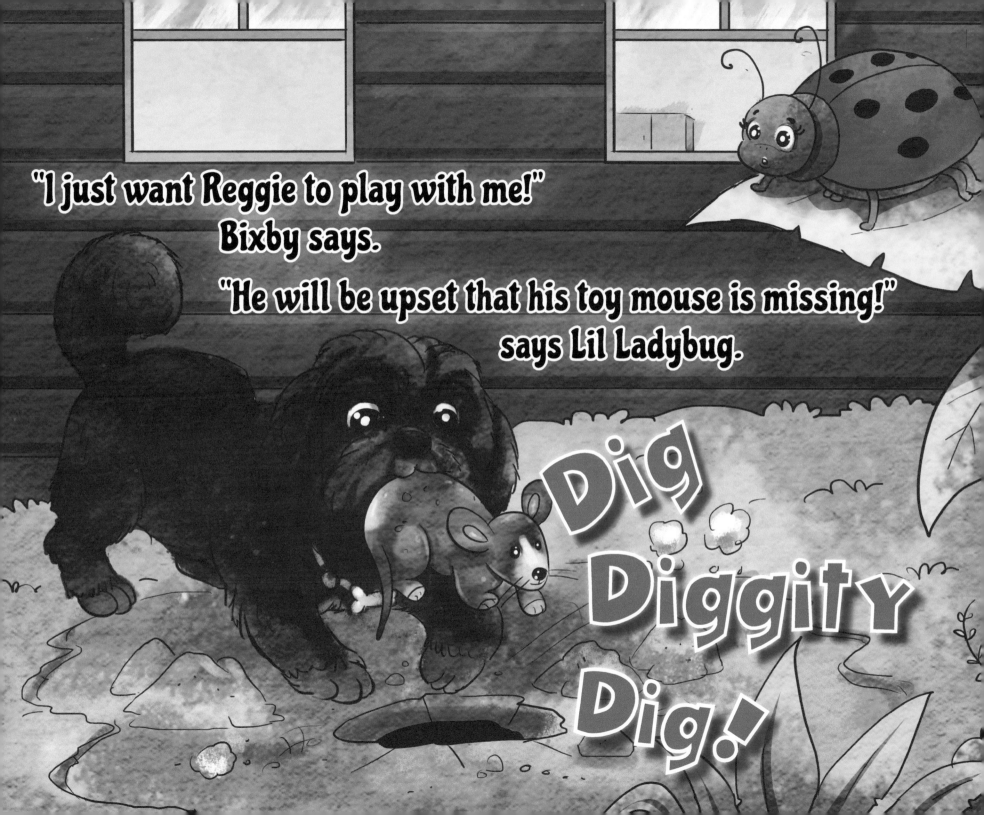

But Bixby just ignores Lil Ladybug.

Inside, Reggie is search, search, searching.
"Where in the world is my toy mouse?" Reggie mews.

Howlelujah, I've got him!

Now Reggie will play with me, Bixby thinks.

Bounce, bounce, bounce!

Bixby goes in for the **pounce!**
But Reggie does not play with Bixby.
Bixby's tummy gives a bigger twinge when he hears Reggie meowing mournfully for his toy mouse.

HARUMPH!

Bixby thinks.
I'll find someone else
to play with.

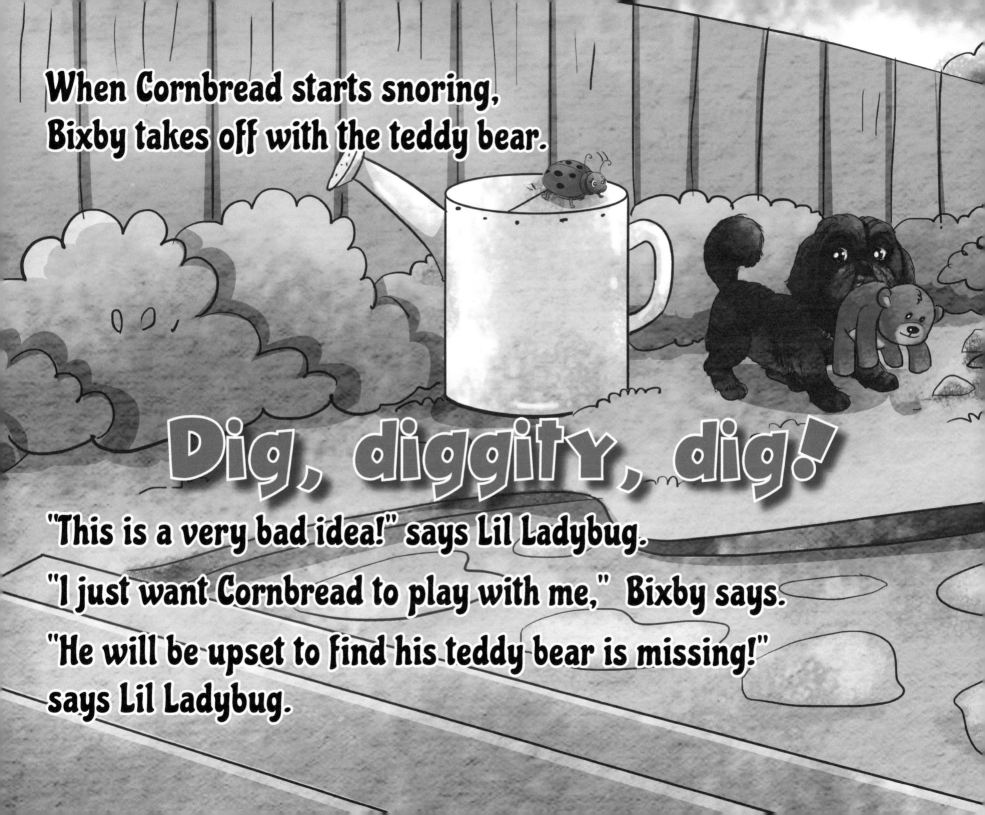

When Cornbread starts snoring,
Bixby takes off with the teddy bear.

Dig, diggity, dig!

"This is a very bad idea!" says Lil Ladybug.

"I just want Cornbread to play with me," Bixby says.

"He will be upset to find his teddy bear is missing!"
says Lil Ladybug.

But Bixby just ignores Lil Ladybug.

Inside, Cornbread is

search,
search,
searching.

"Where in the world is my teddy bear?" Cornbread woofs.

HOWLELUJAH! I've got him!

Now Cornbread will play with me,
Bixby thinks.

Bounce, bounce, bounce!

Bixby goes in for the pounce!

But Cornbread does not play with Bixby.

Bixby's tummy gives an even bigger twinge when he hears Cornbread woofing woefully for his teddy bear.

HARUMPH! Bixby thinks.

I'll go chew on my favorite ball.

But Bixby's ball is nowhere to be found.

"Where in the world is my favorite ball?" Bixby barks.

Bixby search, search, searches for his ball.

He can't find it anywhere!

And then his tummy gives the biggest twinge of all.

Did he make all his friends feel as sad as he is feeling right now?

Bixby wags his tail in agreement.

"And no more tummy twinges!"

ORDER INFORMATION

REDEMPTION PRESS

To order additional copies of this book, please visit
www.redemption-press.com.
Also available at Christian bookstores, Amazon, and Barnes and Noble.

Printed in the USA
CPSIA information can be obtained
at www.ICGtesting.com
LVHW062024141123
763892LV00045B/619